Rumpelstiltskin

Cover illustrated by	Adapted by	Illustrated by
Deborah Colvin Borgo	Sarah Toast	Burgandy Nilles

Louis Weber, C.E.O.
Publications International, Ltd.
7373 North Cicero Avenue
Lincolnwood, Illinois 60646

Permission is never granted for commercial purposes.

Manufactured in U.S.A.

8 7 6 5 4 3 2 1

ISBN: 0-7853-1854-2

Publications International, Ltd.
Story Garden is a trademark of Publications International, Ltd.

Once there was a poor miller who lived with his beautiful daughter. The miller was in the habit of boasting to anyone who would listen of his daughter's great beauty and talents.

One day, on his way to deliver flour to the castle, the miller happened to meet the king. The miller immediately started bragging about his daughter. He told the king that she was the most beautiful, talented maiden in the land.

The king just yawned. The boastful miller was quite determined to have the king notice his daughter. So he bragged on. "I've saved the best for last, your majesty. My daughter can spin straw into gold!"

The king was a greedy man, so he ordered the miller to bring his daughter to the castle. The king took the girl to a room filled with straw and gave her a spinning wheel.

"Now get to work," said the king. "If you do not spin this straw into gold by morning, you will die."

The poor girl knew how to spin flax and wool, but she could not spin straw into gold. She was so frightened that she began to cry. Suddenly the locked door flew open and there stood a strange little man.

"Good evening, pretty maid," he said. "Why are you crying so?"

The miller's daughter told the strange little man that her father boasted to the king that she could spin straw into gold. But since she really couldn't, she must die.

The little man picked up a bit of straw and said that he would have no trouble spinning it into gold.

"What will you give me if I spin this straw for you?" he asked the maiden.

"I will give you my necklace," she replied.

The odd little man took the necklace and sat down at the spinning wheel. He picked up straw and began to spin. By morning all of the spools held spun gold, and the man was gone.

When the greedy king entered the room in the morning, he was greatly pleased to see the gold. That evening the king took the maiden to a bigger room filled with even more straw. Once again he commanded her to spin all the straw into gold if she valued her life.

Locked in the room, the girl sat down and wept. Again the strange little man appeared.

"What will you give me if I spin this straw into gold?" he asked.

"I will give you my ring," she replied.

So the little man took the ring, started the spinning wheel whirring, and by morning he had spun all the straw into bright gold.

The king was still not satisfied. He sent the girl to a much larger room filled with straw to the ceiling. Then he promised to make her his wife if she could spin that straw into gold.

That night the strange little man came for the third time and asked what the girl would give him if he helped her.

"Oh dear," she said, "I have nothing more to give you."

"Then give me your firstborn child when you become queen."

As she did not know what the future held, the maiden agreed. By morning the room was filled with gold. The king married the miller's daughter, and she became queen.

By the time she gave birth to a beautiful child one year later, the queen had forgotten all about the strange little man. But one day he appeared when the baby was sleeping.

"Now give me what you promised," he demanded.

The young queen was horrified. She loved her baby dearly and could not give it up. "I'll give you anything else you want," she cried, "only do not take my child!"

The little man felt some pity for the queen, so he told her, "I will give you three days' time to guess my name. If you can guess it, you can keep your child."

The queen sat up all night making a long list of names. When the little man came to her the next day, she rattled off the list of names.

"Is it Caspar, Melchior, or Balthazar?" she asked.

But for each one the man said, "No, that is not my name."

"Alex, Abraham, Aloysius? Boris, Bruce, or Brian?"

"No, no, and no again!"

The queen read every name she knew, with no luck. As the strange little man left that day he called out, "Only two more days!"

The queen was terribly worried and quickly sent out messengers throughout the country to find other names.

When the messengers returned from their search, the queen wrote a new list of names. The second day she tried them all.

"Could you be Ribcage, Muttonchop, or Lacelegs?"

"No," said the man.

"Nostrin or Houdini? Hercules or Xerxes?"

"Of course not," he said.

When he left, the desperate queen sent her messengers out again. As the very last one was returning to the castle, he came upon a little man dancing around a fire and singing a song.

Today I brew, and then I bake,
And then the queen's own child I'll take.
For little knows my royal dame
That Rumpelstiltskin is my name!

The queen cried out with joy and rewarded the messenger well. The queen prepared a final list of names for the little man, saving his own for last. When the smug little man returned later that day, the queen was ready.

"Is your name Kurt or Bert?"

"No, it is not."

"Underwood or Updike?"

"No, no, no."

"Tom, Dick, or Harry?"

"No! Now give me the baby!" shouted the little man.

"Wait just a minute. I have one final guess," said the queen. "Is your name, by any chance, Rumpelstiltskin?"

The little man was completely amazed and stared at the queen for a long moment. Then he screamed out in rage, "How did you know it? There's no way you could've guessed it!"

The strange little man was so furious that he stamped his feet right through the floor and disappeared forever.